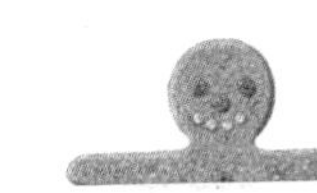

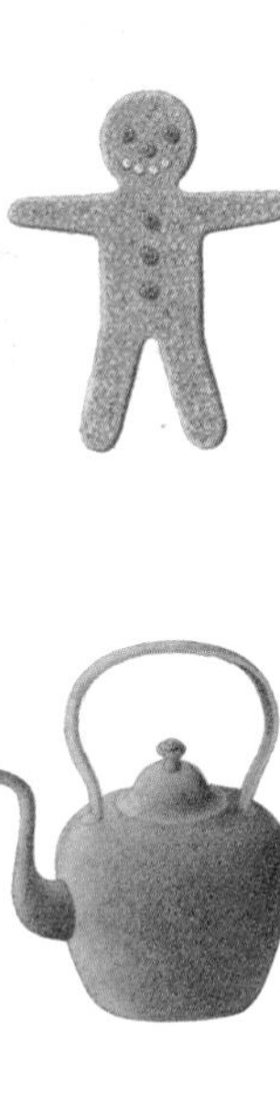

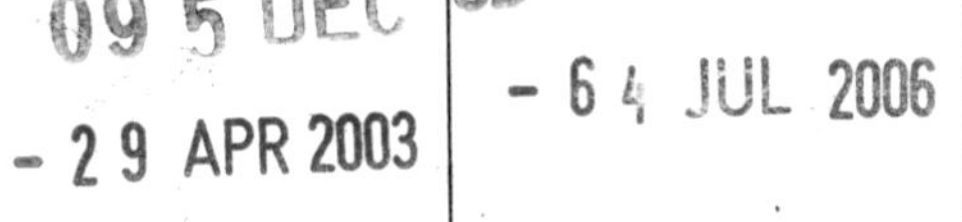

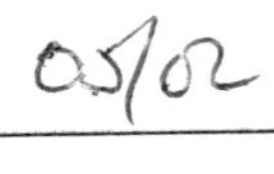
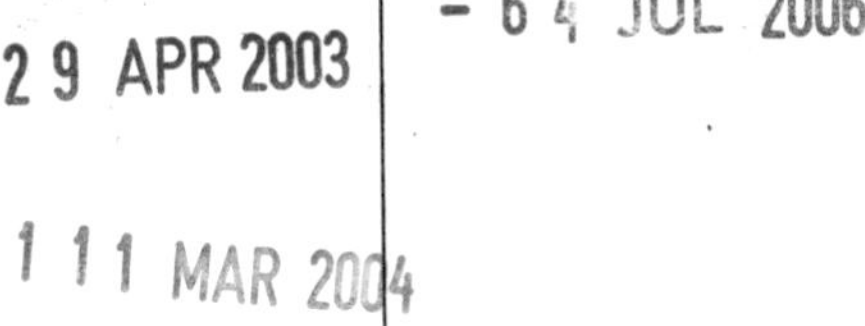

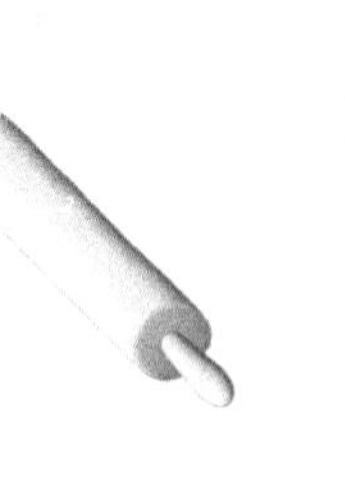

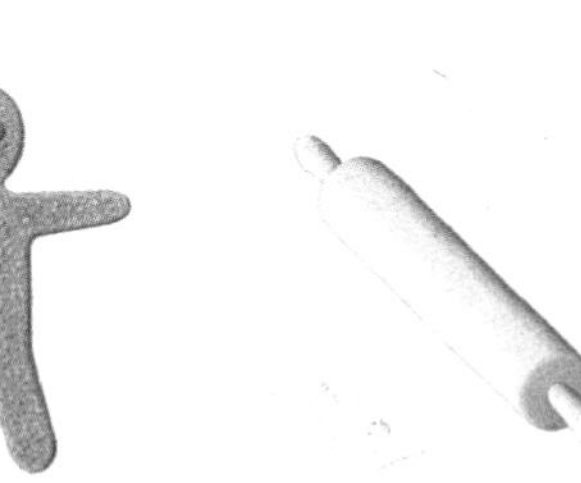

A DORLING KINDERSLEY BOOK

For Benjamin Gardner Miller – BB
To Charles and Samuel – NM

First published in Great Britain in 1998 by Dorling Kindersley Limited,
9 Henrietta Street, London WC2E 8PS

Visit us on the World Wide Web at
http://www.dk.com

A CIP catalogue record for this book is available from the British Library.

ISBN 0-7513-7088-6

Colour reproduction by Dot Gradations
Printed and bound by Tien Wah Press, Singapore

The Gingerbread Man

TOLD BY BARBARA BAUMGARTNER
ILLUSTRATED BY NORMAN MESSENGER

DORLING KINDERSLEY
London • New York • Sydney • Moscow

ONE DAY GRANDMA was baking gingerbread biscuits. She said, "I will bake a little Gingerbread Man!"

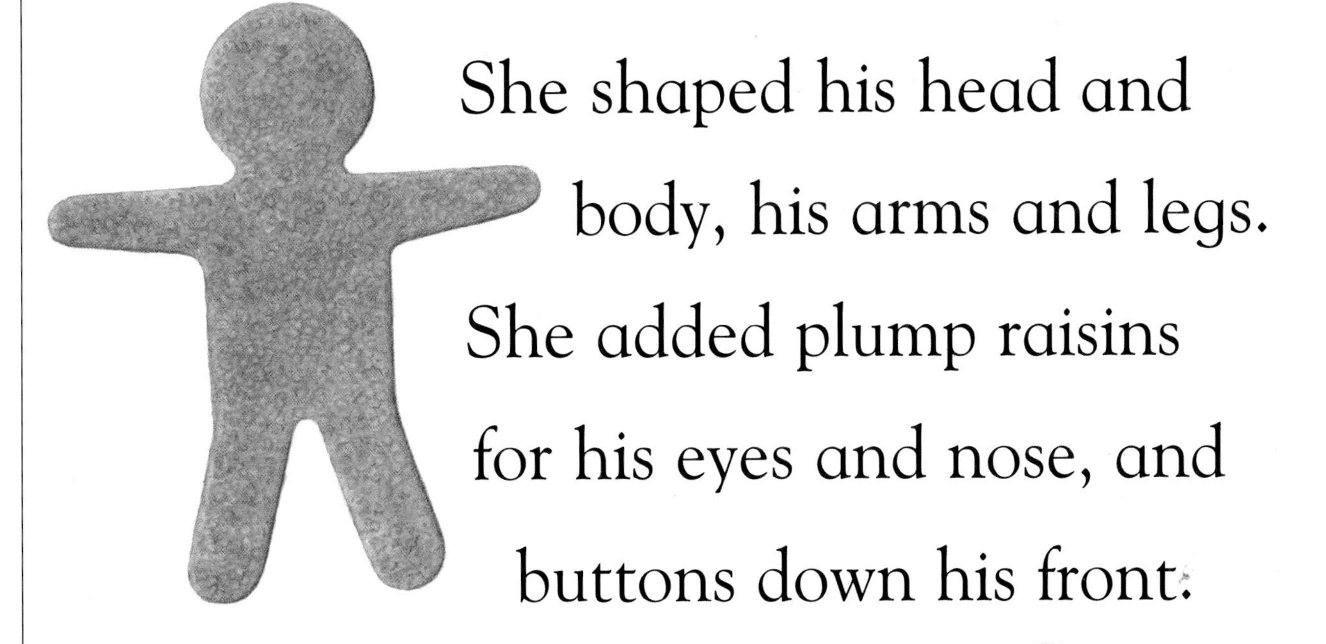

She shaped his head and
body, his arms and legs.
She added plump raisins
for his eyes and nose, and
buttons down his front.

She used little white
sweets for his mouth.
Then she put him in the
oven to bake.

When the Gingerbread Man was crisp and brown, Grandma opened the oven door. But the Gingerbread Man jumped out of the oven and

ran out of the door, singing,

"Run, run

As fast as you can!

You can't catch me –

I'm the Gingerbread Man!"

Grandma ran, but the
Gingerbread Man ran faster.

Soon he came to a duck, who said,

"Quack, quack!

Stop, little Gingerbread Man!

I would like to eat you!"

But the Gingerbread Man
ran on, singing,
"Run, run
As fast as you can!
You can't catch me –
I'm the Gingerbread Man!"

The duck waddled after him, but the Gingerbread Man ran faster.

Soon he came to a cow, who said,

"Moo, moo!
Stop, little
Gingerbread Man!
I would like to eat you!"

But the Gingerbread Man
ran on, singing,

"Run, run
As fast as you can!
You can't catch me –
I'm the Gingerbread Man!"

The cow trotted after him, but the Gingerbread Man ran faster.

Soon he came to a horse, who said,

"*Neigh, neigh!*

Stop, little Gingerbread Man!

I would like to eat you!"

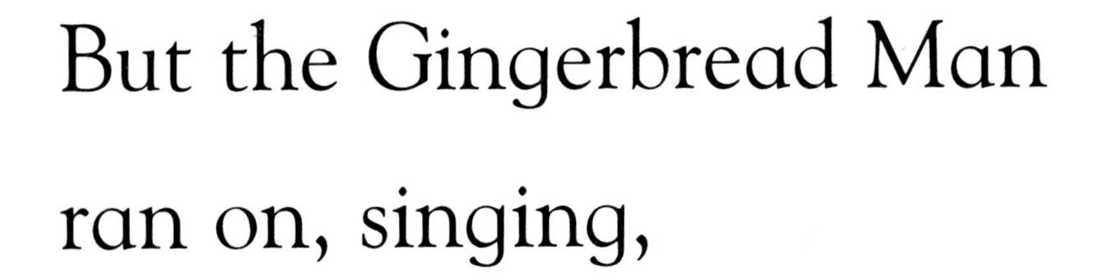

But the Gingerbread Man
ran on, singing,

"Run, run
As fast as you can!
You can't catch me –
I'm the Gingerbread Man!"

The horse galloped after him, but
the Gingerbread Man ran faster.

When the Gingerbread Man looked over his shoulder, he could see everyone running after him.

Grandma called, "STOP! STOP!"
The duck said, "Quack, quack!"
The cow said, "Moo, moo!"
The horse said, "*Neigh, neigh!*"

Then the Gingerbread Man saw a fox sitting near the river. He sang out,

"Run, run
As fast as you can!
You can't catch me –
I'm the Gingerbread Man!"

The sly fox said,
"Gingerbread Man, I'm your friend.
I will help you cross the river.
Jump on my tail."

The Gingerbread Man jumped on
the fox's tail and the fox swam out
into the river.

Halfway across the river, the fox said, "Gingerbread Man, the water is very deep. Hop on my back so you won't get wet."

The Gingerbread Man hopped on the fox's back.

Then the fox said,
“Gingerbread Man, the water is
even deeper. Hop on my head.”

The Gingerbread Man hopped
on the fox’s head.
The fox tossed
his head and

Snip, Snap,

he ate up the

Gingerbread Man.

Like every good biscuit that ever came out of the oven,
the Gingerbread Man was
ALL GONE!